How Babik Cheated Death
A Romani Folktale

A Graded Reader
adapted by Walton Burns
A2+ / **Elementary**

Leveling information	
Word Count	732
Word Tokens	194
Avg. Words/Sentence	8.44
Gunning Fog	4.09
Fleisch- Kincaid Reading Ease	92.86
Fleisch-Kincaid Grade	2.40

all leveling done with
textinspector.com

ISBN: 978-1-7363187-6-8 (print)
978-1-7363187-7-5 (ebook)
Edited by Angela Libal
Illustrations by @van.illustrator.
Map by Alice Hunter, Wikimedia (CC BY-SA 4.0)
For discounts on class sets, contact us:
Alphabet Publishing • 1024 Main St. #172

Branford, CT 06405 • USA

info@alphabetpublishingbooks.com

www.alphabetpublishingbooks.com

Table of Contents

Before You Read

The Romani are very misunderstood. Their traditional lifestyle is different from many other cultures. Many, but not all, Romani travel from place to place. Sometimes other people feared them. They made up mean stories about why Romani traveled. They said the Romani were bad people. Some people said they were from Egypt. This is how they came to be known as "gypsies". But this term is considered an offensive slur. "Romani" is the correct term.

Sometimes other people did terrible things to the Romani, like making them slaves or killing them. Even today, some have negative ideas about Romani people. Some countries want the Romani to abandon their culture and traditions.

However, the Romani people have a rich culture, with strong family and community ties. There are many different Romani tribes. Each tribe has their own traditions. Romani live all over the world, particularly Europe, the US, and Brazil. Romani music is world famous. Their story telling traditions are less well-known. Many stories begin by telling how the storyteller learned about this story. If you are telling a made-up story, like this one, you must make that clear. This can be done directly. It can also be done with humor. Made-up stories can be invented by the storyteller or they can be old, well-known stories. Often the person telling the story invents a new story but use characters and events from other stories. Of course, because the Romani have many tribes, there is no one story-telling tradition. However, the clever hero is a common theme in many Romani folktales, and the story of a person who tricks the devil and goes to heaven is told by many tribes, and even among non-Romani peoples!

One day, an angel came to Earth. He
visited a small village, where a man
named Babik lived. Babik thought, "If
I help the angel, the angel will help
me."

Babik invited the angel home. They had a delicious dinner. Babik and his wife told interesting stories and funny jokes. They gave him a comfortable bed.

In the morning, the Angel gave Babik four wishes, as a reward. Babik was a clever man. He planned his wishes carefully.

This is what Babik wished for:

1. No one can climb down from my apple tree until I let them.

2. No one can get off my rug until I let them.

3. No one can leave my money box until I say so.

4. If I sit on my hat, no one can move me.

The angel gave Babik all his wishes!

Babik lived for many years and had a very happy life. He and his wife had many children!
But he got old.

When he was 70 years old, Death came for him. Death said, "You had a good life, Babik. Now it's time to go."

Babik asked to say goodbye to his family. He told Death to wait in the apple tree. Death climbed the apple tree.

Babik said, "Now you are trapped! Let me live 10 more years. Then you can come down."
Death agreed and Babik let him down

When Babik was 80 years old, Death
came again. Babik was reading a book
by the fire. Babik said, "Let me finish
the book."

Death agreed and sat down on the rug!
Then Babik said, "I tricked you again!
You cannot get up."
Death was very angry but he gave
Babik 10 more years of life.

When Babik turned 90, Death said, "I don't want to go!" So the Devil went for Babik.

Babik asked, "How do I know you are the Devil?"

The Devil changed his body.

He became very big with long sharp horns and long sharp teeth and red eyes.

Babik said, "OK, that is scary. But can you get very small? So small you fit in my money box?"

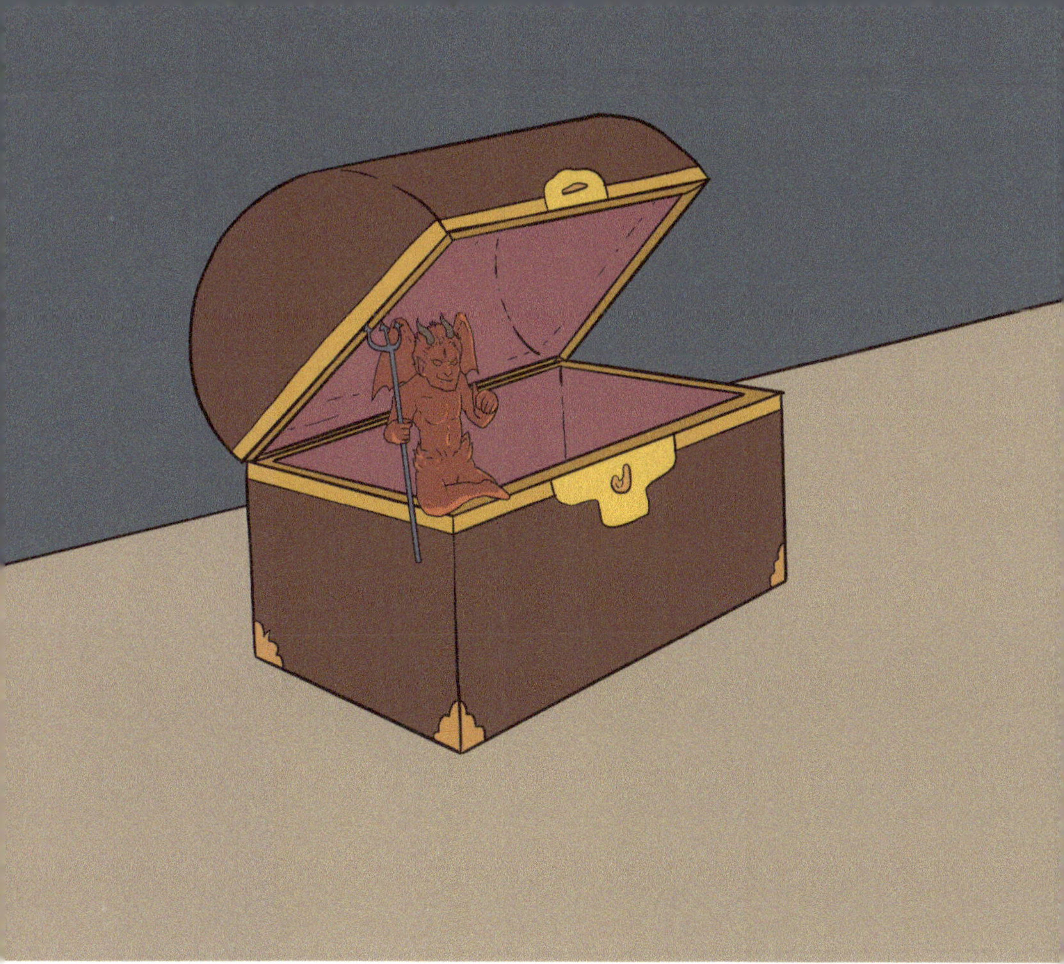

The Devil said, "I can do anything!"
He got very small and he jumped into
the money box.
Babik slammed the top shut.

"I will let you out," he said, "but you must leave me alone. I will decide when I want to leave the world."

The Devil was very angry, but he agreed Babik could live forever.

Babik lived another 10 years. When he was 100 years old, he was very tired. His wife had passed. His children were old.

Babik said to himself, "It is time to go."

So Babik put on his hat and walked to the Devil's cave. But the Devil saw Babik coming. He said, "I don't want you."

So Babik walked to the staircase to Heaven. The angels had heard about Babik. They did not want Babik to trick them too.

So they closed the door to Heaven.
Babik said, "I will leave. Please open
the door for just one second. I just want
to see Heaven."

The angels at the door agreed. They
opened the door. Babik quickly threw
his hat inside and jumped on it.
No one could move Babik now

Someday when you go to heaven, you will go in the door. There you will see Babik, still sitting on his hat!

Vocabulary

slur: a mean word to talk about someone's culture, race, or ethnicity.

to cheat: (*here*) stop someone from getting what they want

angel: a being that serves God, in many religious traditions

to trap: catch someone so that they cannot get away

to trick: make someone do something you want by being clever

The Devil: a powerful evil being, who punishes bad people after they die, in many Christian traditions

to slam: close something quickly so that it makes a loud noise.

staircase: a set of steps

Heaven: the place where God lives and good people go after death in most Christian traditions

Questions

1. Why did Babik help the angel?

2. What wishes did the angel give Babik?

3. How does he use those wishes?

4. Why do you think Babik wanted to continue living on Earth?

5. Why does he finally decide to leave?

6. Why does he try to trick Death?

7. Do you think he is happy at the end?

8. Does this story have a moral or lesson in your opinion?

9. How would you trick Death?

10. What do you think happens to people after they die?

Creating

Many cultures have stories about a trickster. A trickster is a person or animal that tricks or fools people. Sometimes the trickster is bad and hurts the hero. Sometimes they are wise and actually teach a lesson with their tricks. Sometimes they are just very clever or funny.

Do you know a story from your culture about a trickster?

If not, you can make up your own trickster story and write it down or tell it to the class.

Learn More

There are a lot of stereotypes and false stories about the Romani. It is important and interesting to learn the truth about them. Read more about the Romani from online resources, such as the Live Science article at https://www.livescience.com/64171-roma-culture.html.

Pick one part of Romani culture that is interesting to you, such as art, music, clothing, food, beliefs, or something else. You may want to look at one area of the world or one tribe. Learn as much as you can and tell the class what you have learned.

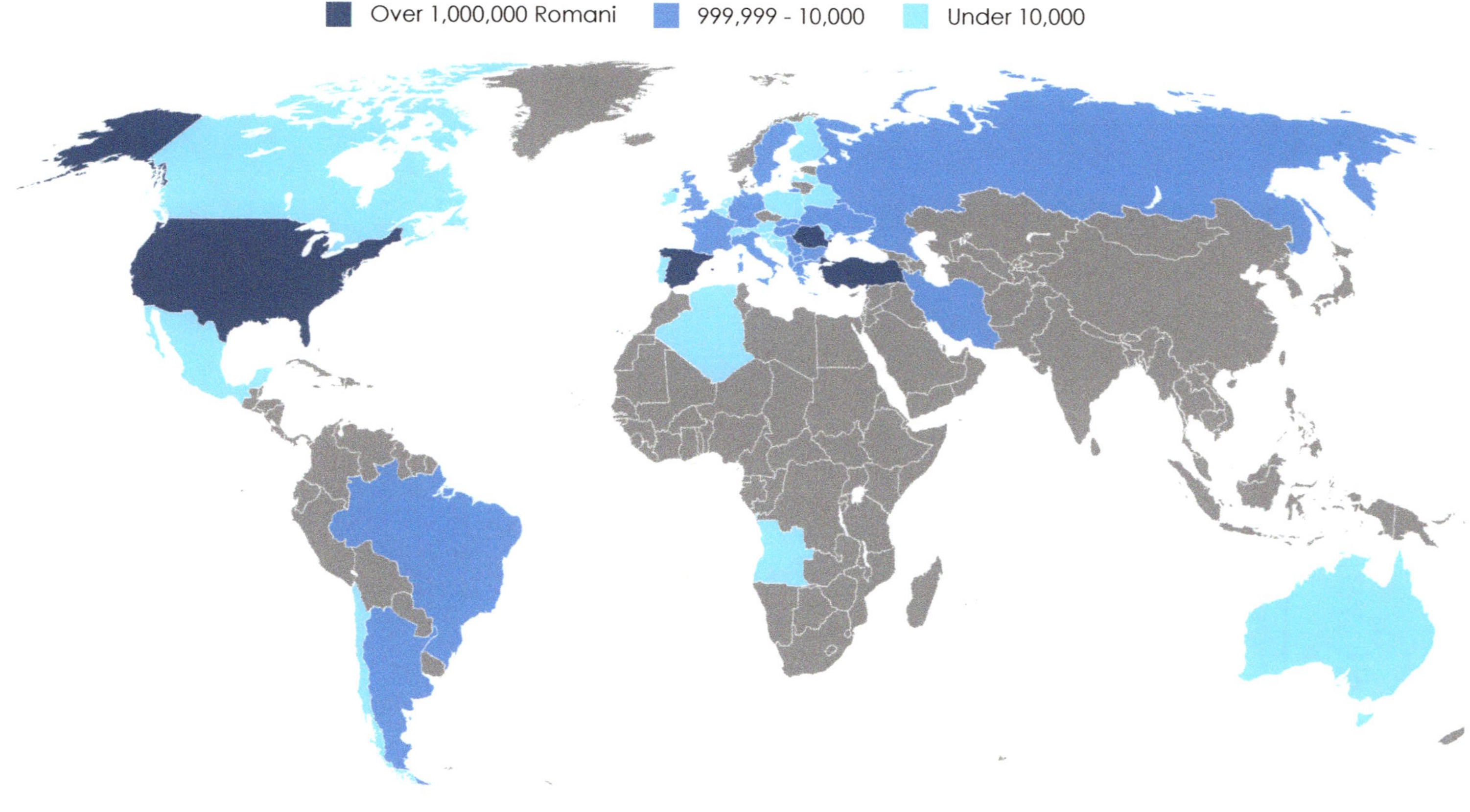

This map shows about how many Romani lived in each country in 2020. Does anything surprise about this map?

Other Graded Reader Titles

The Real Treasure

The Wise Little Girl

The Feast That Stopped a War

How Babik Cheated Death

The Fox and the Magpie

The Freedom Bird

www.AlphabetPublish.Com/Readers